HEARD

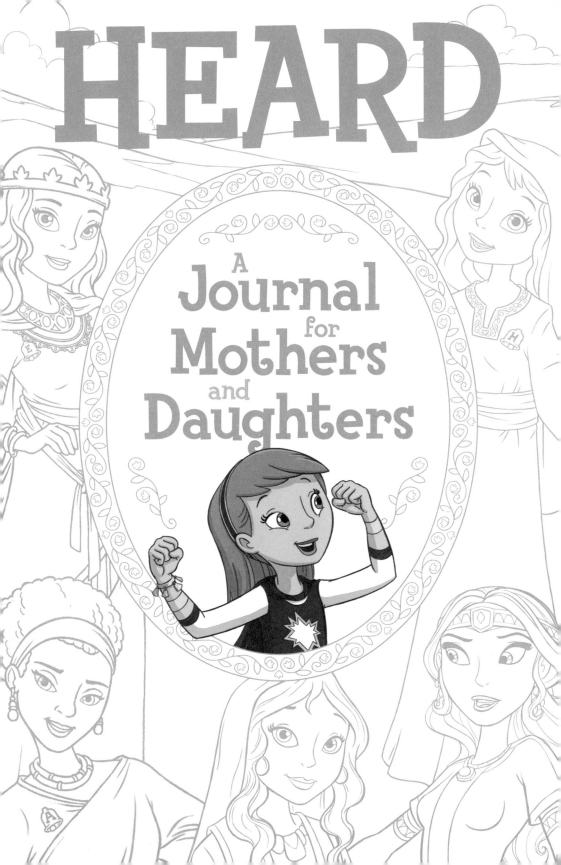

A Journal for Mothers and Daughters

bible ⊕ belles

Text © 2019 by Erin Weidemann

Interior Design by: John Trent
Cover Design by: Ron Eddy & John Trent
Character Illustrations by: Megan Crisp

Manufactured in the United States

Truth Becomes Her
270 N. El Camino Real, #F241, Encinitas, California 92024

978-0-9961689-8-4

TruthBecomesHer.com

This journal
belongs to

and

Your Voice Matters.

Welcome to the HEARD Journal. This interactive journal is the perfect compliment to the Bible Belles series and devotional. In these pages, you will find practical ways to go deeper with the stories of the Belles—Hannah, Esther, Abigail, Ruth, and Deborah—and consider how each one of them *had a unique role to play in God's story*. They used their voices to make a difference. So can you.

This journal offers a safe place to nurture those voices: a shared space for both of you to think and feel deeply that gives you permission to be open, vulnerable, and united in the pursuit of personal growth as well as a strong interpersonal relationship. It includes verses, activities, writing prompts to cultivate connection and free space to record thoughts, feelings, dreams, drawings, and whatever else comes to mind.

When you look back on your life and relationship, what will you see? My prayer is that you close your eyes and revisit memories and moments when you spent time together, with intention, pouring over God's Word and prioritizing the things that truly matter.

Happy journaling!

Erin Weidemann

Table of Contents

Hannah

What I love about the story of Hannah

My favorite part of the story of Hannah is

daughter

My favorite scene

mother

The scene I like best

daughter

free space

free space

free space

free space

Hannah's story is important because

✳

✳

How prayer has impacted my life

✳

✳

✳

Like Hannah, I can pray when I feel

....

....

....

....

✳ ....

....

....

....

What I want to know about talking to God

....

....

....

✳ ....

....

....

....

....

....

daughter

✳

What I thank God for

mother

What I thank God for

daughter

free space

free space

free space

free space

What I often pray about

mother

What I often pray about

The Lord is close to all who call on him, yes, to all who call on him in truth. – Psalm 145:18

What does calling on the Lord *in truth* mean to us?

What can we do together to make prayer a priority?

mother daughter

free space

free space

free space

free space

She is a vessel for honor,
sanctified and useful,
prepared for
every good work.

Esther

What I love about Esther's story

The part of Esther's story I like best

daughter

The scene I like best

mother

My favorite scene

daughter

free space

free space

free space

Esther's story is important because

....

....

....

....

....

....

....

Times I have struggled to be patient

....

....

....

....

....

....

....

....

✳

Like Esther, I can be patient when

....

....

....

....

✳

....

....

....

Times I have struggled to be patient

....

....

✳

....

....

....

....

....

....

✳

Why it's so hard for me to wait

I tend to lose my patience when

daughter

free space

free space

free space

free space

What can I do that will help me remember to be patient and wait on God's timing?

mother

When I need help to practice patience, what can I do?

daughter

Be completely humble and gentle; be patient, bearing with one another in love. - Ephesians 4:2

What do we think *bearing with one another in love* means?

What are some ways we can encourage each other to wait and trust in God's timing?

mother daughter

free space

free space

free space

free space

She knows her God
is in control
and let's that truth
make her brave.

Abigail

Abigail's bravery shines through when she

My favorite part of the Abigail story is when

daughter

mother

daughter

free space

free space

free space

74

free space

What I believe Abigail's story can teach us

✳

....

....

....

....

✳

....

....

....

A time when I let fear stop me from doing something I wanted to do

....

....

....

....

....

✳

....

....

....

✳

Like Abigail, I am brave when

....

....

....

....

✳

....

....

....

....

A time when I let fear stop me from doing something I wanted to do

....

....

....

....

....

....

....

....

....

✳

daughter

Some of the bravest women I know

What I can tell myself the next time I feel scared

daughter

free space

free space

I feel the most brave when

I'm my bravest self when

daughter

Therefore, my dear brothers and sisters, stand firm. Let nothing move you. Always give yourselves fully to the work of the Lord, because you know that your labor in the Lord is not in vain. – 1 Corinthians 15:58

What does it mean that our *labor in the Lord is not in vain*?

mother   daughter

What are some ways we can encourage each other to live boldly
and bravely?

mother daughter

free space

free space

free space

free space

She is more
than a conqueror
through Him
who loves her.

Ruth

Why the story of Ruth is important to me

What I like about Ruth's story

daughter

My favorite scene

mother

The scene from Ruth I like best

daughter

free space

free space

free space

free space

103

What the story of Ruth shows me about loving others faithfully

A time in my life when it was difficult to show love

mother

✴

Like Ruth, I am loyal when I

It's hard for me to love people when

What I've learned over the years about love and loyalty

mother

What I look for in a friend

daughter

What I love about my daughter

mother

What I love about my mom

daughter

free space

free space

free space

A new command I give you: Love one another.
As I have loved you, so you must love one another.
– John 13:34

When Jesus said to love one another *as I have loved you*, what exactly
did He mean?

How can we work together to put the needs of others before our own?

mother daughter

free space

free space

free space

free space

She sets
her mind
on things
above.

Deborah

Why Deborah's story is important for me

mother

What I like best about Deborah

daughter

My favorite scene from the story of Deborah

mother

The scene I like best

daughter

free space

free space

free space

free space

Why Deborah is an example of a great leader

How I feel about my own ability to lead

✻

Like Deborah, I can be a leader when

What I think it means to be a leader

daughter

Someone who inspires me

mother

Someone who inspires me

daughter

free space

free space

free space

139

My dreams for how God wants my girl to lead

The best thing about how my mom leads me

daughter

Sitting down, Jesus called the Twelve and said, "Anyone who wants to be first must be the very last, and the servant of all." - Mark 9:35

What does being a *servant of all* have to do with being a good leader?

How can we support each other to lead lives dedicated to love, sacrifice, and service?

mother daughter

free space

free space

free space

What I've learned from this journal and our time writing in it

mother

What I've learned from this journal and our time writing in it

daughter

free space

free space

free space

free space

free space

free space

free space

free space

157